Haunted Jo

WAVERLY HILLS

Sarah French

&

Joe Knetter

All events and pictures portrayed in this book are our experiences at Waverly Hills Sanatorium.

Also available from Joe Knetter:

Twisted Loneliness

Vile Beauty

Room

Inspired Nightmares

Grave Mistake

Trapdoor

Also available from Joe Knetter and Sarah French:

Haunted Journeys: Salem

"When you have a real paranormal experience it is something that changes you. Sometimes it's better not to know."

Waverly Hills

SANATORIUM

Introduction

Hospitals have always creeped me out. One of the very first horror flicks I remember watching was "Halloween II". As we all know, a good portion of the film takes place in a hospital. As in all of cinema, of course the hospital was dark and deserted. This has always stuck with me, the creepiness and isolation; a perfect place for a monster or killer to lurk. You are in a building where countless people have been helped…but you don't think about that, you think about people dying. How many lied there writhing in pain, waiting for death, embracing it, wanting it? By design hospitals are creepy. The hospital in Minnesota we went to was a Catholic facility. Religious imagery and relics were everywhere. Again, that is supposed to comfort you, but we horror fans always look at things differently. We know that behind a cross is a demon ready to pounce and feed. After experiencing hospitals with Joe and realizing they are never dark and rarely empty I'm still creeped out. Needless to say, ever since watching that film, hospitals have never been the same to me. Thank you John Carpenter! It's important for you to know that because this book deals with a hospital. But not just any hospital, the Granddaddy of them all when it comes to the paranormal. This one is dark and deserted. It's the place where people went to die. There wasn't much in regard to saving there. Just death, so much death, and also some brutal experimental treatments. We can't forget that. For most, going to this place meant the end of the road. Your corpse would make its way down a tunnel, as many other's had.

Welcome to Waverly Hills Sanitarium.

A Brief History

You probably know Waverly Hills Sanatorium for being one of the most haunted locations in the United States of America. The road that led to it earning that moniker was long and dark, very similar to the road that leads up to it.

Thomas Hays purchased the property in Louisville, Kentucky in the year 1883. The home was remote, with no schools nearby. In those days you couldn't just hop on a bus to get around, unless your horse was named Bus. Which was probably rare. Maybe Gus though, that seems to be something you'd call a horse. Look, we are already off topic, but you should expect that coming from us…so back to the history. What do you do in cases like that? Well if you're the Hays family you opened your own school, and that's what they did. It was called Waverley School. Mr. Hays liked the name and named his property Waverley Hills. The name stuck (minus the second "e") when it was purchased and a hospital was built on the grounds. The isolated area was a perfect place to house the patients away from the general population.

Due to the areas moist climate, tuberculosis or TB for short was widespread in the Louisville area and this first wooden structure quickly ran out of room. The hospital went through many renovations attempting to keep up with the spreading disease. More and more patients needed a bed; some even lived outside in a tent. The wood structure deteriorated over time and plans were laid to build a more solid structure that could hold many patients.

The TB epidemic continued and patients were stacked all over the facility. The building you see now was completed in 1926. There is no exact count as to how man lost their lives there, some say upwards of 100,000 but most think it was closer to 20,000. Regardless, it was a heartbreaking outbreak.

The vast amount of people that died daily was the reason they used an underground passageway (the body chute aka the death tunnel) to transport the bodies out of the facility in order to not upset the patients. Some still held hope that they would be saved and fought as hard as they could. Most knew that it was a death sentence.

In 1944 a cure for TB was finally discovered and in the next decade a hospital so massive was no longer needed.

In 1962 it reopened as the Woodhaven Geriatric Center. It was a nursing home used for patients that suffered from advanced mental conditions. It was closed in 1982 due to the rumored mistreatment of patients.

In the latter half of the 1980's it was purchased in order to become a prison, though those plans fell through. It was then going to become condos but that also fell through.

In the 1990's there were plans to make it home to the world's tallest statue of Jesus Christ. That never happened through, thank God. Could you imagine a 150 foot Jesus looking down at you. Somehow that's much creepier than a haunted hospital.

During those years the building fell into disrepair. Windows were smashed, walls fell down, derelicts and the homeless lived there. Drug use was rampant and the building deteriorated into a place no one would ever want to go to.

In the early 2000's it was purchased and became a haunted location open to tours. Many still don't want to go there, but those that do, the open minded paranormal fans, find the place to be a hotspot of activity.

We certainly are those types of people so we set off to Waverly Hills Sanatorium.

INTERSTATE
64
EAST
50
EAST
Louisville

The Road to Darkness

The drive up to Waverly Hills is very creepy. For starters the tours are done overnight, as they should be. It's very dark and quiet. All in all it's exactly what you'd want it to be. It all adds to the ambiance of the experience. Waverly is massive; however you can't see the sanatorium from the road. It's completely covered by the trees. As far as we know, there was only one way up to the place… a dark, dimly lit, rough road. Very few signs marked it, there were more 'no trespassing' signs than anything else.

As we slowly drove up the dark, windy road, covered in trees on both sides, we played King Diamond in the car.

Sarah: Of course we had to get in the mood and what better way to do it, with the King himself.

Joe: "Abigail" is one of my favorite albums of all time. However, for this drive I though "Them" was a more fitting choice and boy was it. Many hate King Diamond for the theatrics, the paint, the over the top storytelling but that's what drew me in. I love King Diamond and play it whenever I can. I once played it as an entrance theme for a reading I did at Cinema Wasteland.

Sarah: Is that the one you did with Sid Haig?

Joe: Yes. We both dressed in Monk outfits. The only light was provided by 20 lit candles. You'd be shocked at how much heat comes off of candles.

Sarah: I'm sure it had nothing to do with the Monk's robes.

Joe: Hush. Let me brag about myself for a bit. It was standing room only. Sid read one of my stories and it was amazing. We passed out signed crosses to a lucky few in attendance. It was most certainly the best reading I ever did. Someday I'll make it back to Cinema Wasteland. I love that show.

Sarah: I never got to go. It would be cool. So any other things you want to plug or brag about?

Joe: I guess it would be pertinent to bring up how losing 75 pounds makes my…

Sarah: Please don't go there. These are the only books you work on that I can show my family.

Joe: You can show them the other ones.

Sarah: I could, but I want them to like you and not think you are batshit crazy.

Joe: But I am batshit crazy.

Sarah: I know. And also r…

Joe: Nope. If I can't talk about my penis you can't talk about…you know.

Sarah: Deal.

Joe: Is it bizarre that as we are writing this, the IPod, which is on shuffle, just played three King Diamond songs in a row?

Sarah: I'm not sure if it's bizarre or a coincidence. You have every album on the IPod.

Joe: That's an astute observation.

Sarah: Should we get back to, you know, the book.

Joe: That's also an astute…

Sarah: Hush.

So we were driving up to Waverly. We were very excited since it is listed as one of the top ten most haunted locations in the US. From what we'd heard about the place, it's a gold mine for spiritual activity. And as we stated in the first book, we love history as much as the paranormal and this place was dripping with it.

Joe: I interrupt this book on Waverly to mention our book on Salem. I'm hoping you read that also. It is a good introduction to what we do with this book series.

Sarah: If this is the first one they've read they are probably thinking the books are about pimping out our shit and things we like.

Joe: Well that's the truth. We love the paranormal and the history. There's plenty of Waverly to come. If this is your first, these books are meant to come across as a conversation. If you know us personally, you'll hear our voices in your head.

Sarah: As opposed to the voices in your head Joe.

Joe: What are you talking about? Yes, I concur, what is she talking about? ?tuoba gniklat uoy era tahW

Driving up this dark, dreary road, we were all quiet, waiting for impending doom.

Sarah: We should mention we were taking the trip with two of our friends. Justin "Sonny" Peterson and Veronica Manahan.

Joe: Veronica was more of a sister to me growing when we were young. We were always together. Walking around the trailer park. Swearing. Walking through the woods behind the school to Cub foods. Rocking the fuck out of the cake walks. Swimming. Going to the shelter when there was a threat of a tornado. We were badass kids.

Sarah: Anything else you want to share about your youth?

Joe: One time I fucked her Dayton's Santa bear.

Sarah: TMI.

Joe: Sonny is a great friend we've known for years. It's also important to mention he didn't believe in the paranormal at all. I should also mention that Sarah and I made a music video for his old band "The Gravities."

Sarah: It's on YouTube. The song is called Parkway Avenue and it's awesome.

Joe: Oh so now you'll turn this into a promo for something.

Sarah: Yeah.

Joe: I'm sure it doesn't have anything to do with the fact that you star in it.

Sarah: Of course not. ☺

Joe: Holy shit. I didn't expect that smiley face to come up. That's creepy as fuck.

Sarah: Can we talk about Waverly?

The investigations are held from 12am to 8am, but they usually want you there a little early to go through a mini-orientation/meet and greet with the other guests and volunteers. It was about 11:30pm when we arrived. We slowly pulled up to a gated fence, at the end of the road. We passed a few homes on the way up and wondered what it would be like to live so close to Waverly.

Sarah: During this time we lived next to a cemetery and know how creepy that was at times. So I can only imagine what it would be like to be so close to a place like that.

Joe: Yes. But that's going to be the next book. We'll promo that later.

Sarah: The next book is about the house in Rochester Minnesota?

Joe: Absolutely.

Sarah: When did we decide that?

Joe: Right now.

There are a few cars in front of us parked, waiting for someone to open the gate. We park the car behind the others and turn up the King (Diamond not Presley). The four of us sit there and take in our surroundings. Pitch black night, lonely old road, trees all around us… yeah, straight out of a horror flick.

Sarah: I was just waiting for Jason to come running out of the woods wielding his machete at us…it was only a matter of time.

Joe: What if he had an axe instead?

Sarah: It would kill you just the same.

Joe: Kill me? What about you?

Sarah: I can run faster than you.

Joe: Of course you can. But I wouldn't run.

Sarah: I know. That's why you'd die.

Joe: I would for you.

Sarah: Awe. How sweet.

Joe: I'm getting some tonight.

While we were waiting for someone to open the gate, we decided to get out of the car. The people in front of us had done the same thing.

Joe: It's best to size up everyone. Let's face it, some people that like to go to places that were the scenes of unspeakable horror and misery are a little off their rocker.

Sarah: Everyone on the tour was cool though.

Joe: I guess that means we were the weirdoes in the group.

We stood there looking towards the woods, in the direction of this massive sanatorium. We couldn't help but think about all the people that suffered from the horrible disease, tuberculosis, over the years. I can't even begin to imagine the totality of what when on there. The fact that they had to build a "body chute" because so many people were dying each day, they needed to hide that so they could keep the morale up… heartbreaking.

About 10-15 minutes pass and we see a car driving down this path towards us, from the other side of the gate. They get out and open the gate from their side. The cars start pulling ahead. The worker stands there on the driver's side and greets people with a clipboard in hand. It had everyone's names on it and one by one she checks them off. Once we get through check in at the gate, we slowly start driving up this windy, dimly lit road. We see a few cars in front of us, they turn, and disappear. The excitement is growing and so is the fear, as we get closer and closer. We slowly get up the hill and slightly turn a corner. There it is, right in front of us…Waverly Hills Sanatorium.

It's a massive red and white brick building with many windows that looks like it goes for miles. As we drive left to park, we pass a "KEEP OUT" sign greeted by a massive Gargoyle next to it.

Sarah: I thought to myself, this is it…tonight we're going to die.

Joe: I have to admit, even I felt a little creeped out. And usually my machismo easily overpowers that before it has a chance to dig in.

Sarah: Machismo…

Joe: I'm practically dripping with it.

Sarah: Is that why you sweat so much?

Once we park, we get out and start suiting up for the investigation. We wanted to make sure we had everything we needed for an eight hour investigation. Each investigation is different in regards to what we bring. For Waverly these are some items and things we knew we needed to have for the long night ahead of us:

- Sneakers: For walking, need to be safe and comfortable. It is an old, decrepit building and there is no power at night. The only light that exists on its own comes from the moonlight creeping in through the broken windows.
- Pants: These are a must for old places like this. We don't want any creepy crawlers getting in any cracks!

- Long sleeve T-shirt/Hoodie: Because it's the middle of the night the temperature drops. You need to stay warm and if need be, it's easy to take off. You only want to feel the chills of the paranormal.
- Camera Bag/Backpacks: To keep everything in.
- Water/Snacks: Keeps us going throughout the night. It's tiring to do these investigations. You need to stay hydrated and full of energy. Especially since most investigations involve sitting and waiting. You don't want to fall asleep.
- Digital Voice Recorder: To try and get some EVPs (Electronic Voice Phenomenon).
- Night Vision Camera: It's dark after all. We have an old one, not the highest quality, but it's better than nothing. Note to self, pick something else up.
- Digital Camera
- Headphones

- Flashlight: There's no electricity inside, so no lights. If we don't want to die, a flashlight is key. Luckily for us it was close to a full moon that night, so that helped (and helped with the creepy factor too)!
- Kid's toy ball: We've did some research beforehand and on the 5th floor, the children's wing, it's said to be haunted by a little boy named Timmy. He likes to play with people, so we wanted to bring him a gift in hopes to communicate. We bring balls to every investigation.

Joe: Yeah we do.

Sarah: Oh boy. I stepped right into that one.

As we suit up outside the car, other cars start to pull in, but not many. I think there was a total of seven cars. I thought that was kind of weird considering this place is usually busy with overnight investigations. But at the same time I just figured we were early and more would show up later. The four of us start to walk towards a smaller building off to the side of the sanitarium. It's the office/gift shop. That's where we will have the official check in and meet and greet. As we walk by the sanitarium towards the office, it's quiet. So quiet we only hear our footsteps on the gravel road. No birds, bugs, nothing.

Sarah: I'm surveying the building as we walk by and just think to myself, I can't believe I'm actually here. I've watched numerous Ghost Hunters episodes to know what we'd be in for. This place is no joke.

We get inside and are greeted by the lady who runs it, along with some volunteers to take us around. We also start to meet the other people who've paid to be there investigating as well. Once the greeting of everyone was done, we had a little time to look around the gift shop. Lots of cool goodies with Waverly all over them…t-shirts, hats, hand bags, magnets, you name it, they had it. They also had a cute kitty lying in a cat bed on the counter. She was sleepy.

Sarah: I'm sure it was her bedtime considering it was so late at night.

Joe: I kind of wanted to hop in the bed for a quick nap.

Sarah: We had driven all day and planned on taking a nap before heading to Waverly.

Joe: We were far too excited to sleep though. Even you couldn't nap and you can sleep anywhere.

Sarah: I was really excited…and also nervous.

Soon after looking around, we're told to have a seat in front of this projection screen. It was weird looking around at all the empty chairs. It was kind of creepy and realization really began to dawn. We we're at Waverly Hills Sanatorium. Soon we would be stepping foot inside. We were excited and felt mild trepidation.

As we looked around, there were only thirteen or so of us on this tour.

Sarah: No one else showed up like I thought they would.

Joe: Usually there are many more people on the tour. I'm not sure how we got so lucky to be in such a small group but we were thrilled.

Sarah: The more people investigating means the more chances for you to catch things that are not paranormal. We try to debunk everything first and that can be difficult with dozens of people in the same property.

Joe: Waverly is massive. In big buildings sometimes sound can carry a long ways. Footsteps on another floor can echo and seem to be coming from next to you. It's always a challenge when there's a big group. There always seems to be one that think's everything is paranormal.

Sarah: And one that thinks it's funny to make shit up and try to joke around.

Joe: Both are people you don't want to investigate with.

Sarah: We were so lucky.

It was a small group of us. Once seated, they give us a little speech welcoming us and start playing a video. It gave the history of Waverly, a rundown of the building, and what transpired there. It was very informative.

Joe: We always research the sites ahead of time in order to go into it with as much knowledge as possible.

Sarah: It's also a good way to see if the hosts are embellishing things at all. In most cases, there is a little of that. They are a business trying to make money after all. In this case the video was accurate to what we had read.

Once the video ended, they handed us each a pass that said Waverly Hills tour admission pass. We needed these passes to enter Waverly.

Before we got going, they explained how the investigations go.

Sarah: Typically they split into groups and you spend time on each floor before moving to the next. You have a guide with you that helps with the investigation and leads you around. You have a limited time on each floor.

Joe: Since our group was so small they gave us the option to explore the building separately. Go where we wanted, when we wanted, on our own. They had volunteers on hand to answer and assist us with any questions we might have.

Sarah: It was the perfect situation. Exploring on your own is so much better. There's no set timeframe. Anyone who does this knows you can't put a timer on it.

Joe: It would be awful to be capturing something and then have to move to another floor.

Sarah: We were so lucky.

There are five floors total, including the body chute, so plenty of room to explore and not be bothered by the other people investigating. As we enter Waverly, through a door in the gift shop, we hand them our passes. They take our passes, one by one, and we enter darkness. No electricity what so ever. If you didn't have a flashlight, they give you one.

Sarah: Of course we had to get some because they say Waverly on them, which we still have to this day!

The volunteer had all of us follow him, single file down a long hallway. We all get to a main room on the first floor. He shows us where the stairs are to access each floor. People start heading in all directions. The guide asks us if we want to go to some of the hot spots of the sanatorium, where people catch most of the activity.

Joe: Always give the guides a chance to show you around at first. It helps you learn the layout.

Sarah: Plus they are there often, so they tend to know the best spots to go.

Joe: With that being said, always be cognizant that in some places they set up things. While we didn't experience that at Waverly other places have done this.

Sarah: Use common sense. If they lead you somewhere and shit immediately starts happening, it's probably a set up. Spirits don't punch a time clock and if it seems that way, it's probably not real.

Since this was our first time there, and we were unsure of where to start, it was a good idea to have our own guide, at least to start out with. Of course we wanted to see the hot spots of this massive place. We had our own guide and he's been a paranormal investigator for many years. He loves what he does and you could tell, was a very cool, no bullshit type of guy. This is where our investigation of Waverly Hills Sanatorium would start and for our friend Sonny, where his belief in the paranormal would begin.

The 4th Floor

Shadow People

The building is pretty run down, as you'd expect, so you had to be careful where you walked. Holes in walls, paint chipping, graffiti, rusted out windows/railings, holes in ceiling, you name it, so you had to be very careful what you touched and where you sat. We get up to the 4th floor after climbing these steps that felt like they went on forever.

The higher we went up, the heavier it felt.

Joe: We discussed this in the last book and will point it out again. Most the time when you experience something paranormal, it's not what you see, it's what you feel.

Sarah: A feeling of heaviness is usually a sign that there's something going on.

Joe: With that being said, quite often you explore old buildings. They are dirty, dusty, maybe not exactly completely free of asbestos and the like. It can make breathing a little more difficult. Many times that's what it is. So you have to use your own judgment in order to differentiate.

Sarah: Plus you tend to be a little nervous and on edge. That can make you feel all sorts of weird.

Joe: Speaking of feeling something weird…

Sarah: Stop touching yourself.

We entered this long, dark hallway. All you could see was open doorways to the left and right with moonlight spilling in from the left side doorways. As we're standing there, flashlights in hand, it was very quiet. We were all just soaking the surrounding in, getting a feel for the place.

Joe: Until you step into the place you really have no concept of how big it is.

Sarah: While the building isn't abandoned, it sure felt like it. I could imagine people living there, feasting on rats and whatever they could get their hands on.

Joe: I would eat you first.

Sarah: Isn't that what you always do?

Joe: Holy shit. That's pretty fucking good. I've taught you well.

Sarah: What can I say? You rubbed off on me.

Joe: Yes I have, I thought you were sleeping though.

Sarah: That's only when we have sex.

Joe: Now they will think I'm a pervert.

Sarah: Okay, I start awake…just fall asleep during.

Joe: They call that passing out from pleasure baby.

Sarah: Uhh…um…sure.

The volunteer told us to turn our flashlights off and let our eyes adjust to the darkness. This was the best advice we've been given. It's natural to want to use a flashlight to see things. I think that's why things are usually missed. The human body is amazing. It adapts very well to its surroundings.

Your vision is no different. Let it settle into the darkness. It only takes a few minutes before you can begin to see what's in front of you.

Sarah: I was hesitant at first, of course, and the goosebumps started to come to me. I turned to Joe with that worried look on my face and he tells me it's going to be okay.

Joe: I lied to her. I didn't know if it was going to be okay. For all I knew something was going to come out and take her away.

Sarah: Thanks for that.

Joe: In hindsight though you were fine…so I didn't lie. I take that back. I knew she'd be okay, with me by her side.

Sarah: So I turned my flashlight off along with everyone else. The five of us stood there in the dark for a few minutes, though it felt like it lasted forever.

Slowly our eyes started to adjust to the darkness. It didn't take long, the moonlight definitely helped with that as well. You are able to see the walls, the doorways, everything within the darkness. The building is in rough shape. Walls are broken, windows long destroyed. Dirt is on the floor along with various things left over the years.

Sarah: If you would have said we'd be walking through Waverly with no lights I would have laughed and told you "no way". But that's what happens. Once your eyes adjust you can move around pretty well in the dark.

Joe: You still have to be very careful though. There are always things to trip on, holes you don't see and then there are the bugs. I fucking hate bugs. Detest them. Spiders are the worst.

Sarah: When you go into an old building, one that has been left deteriorating for quite some time, you're going to find bugs. There's no avoiding it.

Joe: I fucking hate spiders.

Sarah: I know. You said that.

Joe: No, I mean I really fucking hate them. When I was in my teens I got bit by a spider. Right on my scrotum. That dirty, hairy fuck (spider not scrotum) was on the bed when I turned the lights on. I fucking hate them. I know, they eat other bugs…I get that, but I still hate them. So I always recommend using a flashlight when you first enter a room. Look around, make sure you aren't sitting in a nest of spiders. Most are harmless, but there are some really nasty ones.

As we're standing there adjusting our eyes, the volunteer told us to look all the way down the hallway towards the end. Let me add, there was no one else on this floor at the time. We were the first group to explore the upper levels. Everyone else went down to where the body chute was. As we're looking down this long hallway, we start to see something. Little movements so quick that you can barely register it as anything more than a blink. We were unable to catch any of this on camera. The guide let us know that we were looking at Waverly's infamous shadow people.

Joe: I saw it first. Multiple black figures dart back and forth through the different doorways down the hall. Most are very small. One to two feet tall. They aren't humanoid in shape, just quick black blurs darting across the hallway.

Sarah: As Joe is seeing this, he describes what he sees to us. I'm not going to lie. I was freaked out.

Joe: Both Veronica and Sonny began to see what I was seeing.

Sarah: I can't see much because I was wearing my glasses, which I normally only wear when I'm driving, so my eyes couldn't adjust properly in the darkness. Even if I took them off I'd only see blurs, so unfortunately I didn't get the chance to see much.

These shadows moved back and forth for a few minutes before they seemed to stop.

Joe: It was then that I saw something I've never forgotten. Sonny saw it too so I know I didn't imagine it. A large black mass, this one human in shape, stepped out of a doorway and stood still. I could feel it looking at us.

Sarah: The thing to always remember when dealing with the paranormal is, if you can see it, it can see you. It knows you know.

Joe: It stared at us for what seemed like an eternity. In actuality it was only ten seconds or so but it felt so long. It felt like everything else stopped. It was just us and the shadow person.

Sarah: Part of me is glad that I didn't see it. I'm not sure I could have continued all night.

Joe: You would have. I know you.

Sarah: You're probably right.

Joe: Besides, where the fuck would you have gone?

Sarah: I would have gone back and played with the kitty.

Joe: How would you have gotten back to the hotel? A cab?

Sarah: I didn't say I would go back to the hotel.

Joe: I see. You pervert. You would have played with your kitty there. How come you won't have sex in a haunted location but will masturbate?

Sarah: I would play with the cat in the gift shop.

Joe: Oh. My bad.

A few minutes pass by and the volunteer says to us, "Okay, now let's go to the end of this hallway where we saw the shadow people." As paranormal investigators, of course we wanted to check it out and see what was down there.

Sarah: But at the same time I'm silently freaking out! Go where the shadow people are. Where the big one was staring at us? Okay, why not right? Where 90% of people would've said hell no, we were heading straight into the storm.

As we walk down this hallway towards the end, we look through the doorways, taking pictures, and soaking it all in. There is so much sadness and heartbreak in this building. It seems to permeate in each inch of the place. You can't help but think about the history of this place while walking around.

When we get to the spot that we saw the shadow people we spend quite some time looking around. We walked back and forth, room to room, on each side of the hallway, trying to find a reason for what we saw. There are no lights, nothing outside that is casting off shadows, let alone ones that move.

Joe: This is the first time in my life that I saw the shadow people. I was sure I would debunk it. While I believed in the paranormal, I still held the belief that almost all of it is bullshit. But no matter how many times I went over it and looked, there was nothing that screamed fake. And that was just for the random small shadow shapes that were moving around. That's not even talking about the big one. The one that looked like a human. The one that stared at me. The one that knew.

Sarah: We couldn't debunk it. We moved around trying to cast our shadows but it didn't work. So we moved on down the hall.

The Operating room

We got to the end of the hallway and the volunteer had us enter a room. Overall it's pretty small, maybe the size of a bedroom. We all take a seat on the floor, but first, look around and make sure we don't sit on any creepy crawlies.

Joe: I will not let those duplicitous fucks bite my scroats again. Over the years I've developed strength in my sack. I will crush those bastards with my manliness.

Sarah: Uh…um…uh…I have no words.

It's very quiet in the room. Again we are thankful that the groups touring are very small.

Sarah: I look around as I sit there. I see a very old light above us. It looks like a medical light from the mid 1900's.

Sarah: Also attached to the wall is some rusted metal box type thing with old knobs and wires on it. Not really sure what it was but it looked like it had something to do with medical examinations.

The volunteer proceeds to tell us about the room. The room we were sitting in was one of the operating rooms. When the tuberculosis epidemic hit, they had no cures at the time. TB was a death sentence. They did what they could do to make it as comfortable for the patients as possible.

Sarah: But they also did more to some. In trying to find a cure they began to try new ways to help.

Joe: New ways to help? That's a nice way to say they got all medieval.

Sarah: They operated on people. Different experiments to see what would work and what wouldn't.

Joe: It was exactly that, experiments.

These people were basically their guinea pigs for finding cures for tuberculosis. Some of the experiments included rolling out patients to the open patio for "fresh air" and "sun", even when it was raining and snowing, thinking that fresh air could possibly help them. They also tried ultra violet light, opening up patients and using light to stop the spread of bacteria. Another experiment they tried was to surgically removing ribs and muscles from patients in hopes to give their lungs more room to expand. Balloons were also inserted in hopes to expand the lungs. So many brutal attempts that would have caused death to the person regardless of the condition.

Joe: Imagine it. Your chest is cut open, rib cage separated, left that way in hope that you'd be able to breath better. It's absolutely amazing that in this day and age these sort or procedures were done. With no cure in sight they resorted to trying anything. I'm sure in their minds these people were going to die anyway and they were correct, but it just seems like such a brutal chance to take.

Sarah: Nothing worked. TB was a grueling and horrific way to die.

As we sat there, the volunteer takes out a small flashlight from his pocket and sets it on a shelf, across the room from us, pointing it in our direction.

Joe: It needs to be a small mag-light style flashlight, the kind where you twist the top to turn it on.

Sarah: The key is to twist it so it's just barely off.

He set it down and sat next to us. He asked us if we've ever used a flashlight to communicate with spirits. At the time we'd never done anything like that before. We mainly just used digital photography and voice recorders. We were pretty novice at the time, just getting into doing our own paranormal investigations. The flashlight was new to us but we had seen it done before on different TV shows. In theory the spirit can use its energy to make the final connection and turn the flashlight on. If there is something there, and it wants to communicate, they don't need much energy to make the light turn on. It's a tool to help communicate.

Sarah: To start you ask if any spirit would like to talk. You instruct them to use their energy to turn on the light. Then you wait.

Joe: You can usually tell when a spirit is there. You feel the hairs stand up on your arms.

Sarah: Not your arms though, since you shave them now.

Joe: Just to be clear, it isn't a metrosexual type of thing. I shave my arms to better show my tattoos. The hair tends to make them not look as crisp.

Sarah: Sure.

Joe: I'm sorry but that's the truth. A tattoo artist once said to me, "Tattoos are art. They are meant to be seen in the best way possible. Would you buy a painting and hang a curtain over it?

Sarah: For you it would be more of a rug, a shag rug.

Joe: I won't deny that. But you can't deny they look much better with the hair gone.

Sarah: Yes they do.

Joe: Anyway, like I said, if you have the ability to sense spirits, which I think we all do, we just don't allow ourselves to feel it, then you can tell when there is one around. I usually let the spirit know that I know it's there and to communicate with us. When it chooses to the light comes on.

Sarah: You should always be respectful and thank them if they choose to come forward. The best way to use the light is to ask yes or no questions. Instruct them to turn the light on for a yes.

Joe: There is quite a bit of doubt as to the validity of the flashlight communications. I'll share my thoughts about it after we let you know what happened at Waverly Hills.

The volunteer begins to ask questions.

"Is there someone here with us? I can feel you and we saw you in the hallway. Please come forward and communicate. We think that's so cool when you do."

A few minutes pass in silence. We sit and wait. All of a sudden the light starts to slowly flicker on.

"If you're here with us, shine that light nice and bright," the volunteer says.

The light lit up super bright.

"Thank you very much, now step away from the flashlight and turn it off."

A few seconds go by and the light starts to dim and flicker, then it turns off.

Sarah: Yup, at that point I was dumbfounded and so were Joe, Sonny and Veronica.

Joe: This was the first time seeing this in person. My immediate response was to try to debunk it. But I needed to wait until it was over. I didn't want to be rude.

Sarah: Of course you didn't. Now I suppose you'll tell the Joel Robinson story.

Joe: So if you don't know, Joel Robinson is a fantastic artist. He's been doing quite a few Blu Ray covers the last few years and they are amazing. We were at Rock and Shock a few years ago and drinking the Lynchburg Lumberjacks.

Sarah: Gross.

Joe: A Lynchburg Lumberjack is maple syrup and whiskey. Lynchburg comes from Jack Daniels…but we weren't drinking Jack Daniels. Only the best for us. We were drinking Old Crow.

Sarah: Gross.

Joe: So Nick Principe(Chromeskull) and I ended up in Joel's room at 4 in the morning. We were drinking vast amounts of booze and of course the Lynchburg lumberjacks were included.

Sarah: Gross.

Joe: It's not as bad as you'd think. Anyway we were all pretty fucked up. Nick was telling a story and it was very interesting. I had to piss something fierce and tried to hold it until he was done. I knew I couldn't wait any longer so I got up, took two steps and pissed in Joel Robinson's hotel garbage can.

"What are you doing?" Joel asked, realizing what I was doing.

"Nick's telling a story. I don't want to be rude," I replied.

So I think that shows my character.

Sarah: Gross.

The light turned on and off when asked at different times throughout the process. It's one of those things you have to see to believe. We were in that room for about 45 minutes communicating with whatever was in there with us. From what we learned, it was a male that was a patient, but it wasn't the black mass that we saw earlier in the night. This energy we were talking with back and forth told us the black mass was evil and to stay away from it. Towards the end it told us we needed to leave. At that point we didn't hesitate and we started to make our way back to the staircase. The volunteer told us he had this interaction with what was in that room many times and it wasn't a bad energy, but the black mass that roamed the hallways was evil…they name him "the creeper" and he doesn't like the guests that come to visit.

Sarah: Glad he told us this after the fact or else I wouldn't have gone up there!

Joe: Yes you would have. You have more guts than you give yourself credit for.

Sarah: I don't know. I hate messing with anything that's evil. But I am glad we went up there. While I didn't see the shadow people you guys saw, I definitely experienced the flashlight communication.

Joe: Okay so here's the deal with the flashlight. Many people debunk it and I understand why. In theory, if the light is on for a short period of time before you set it down and have it off, when it cools it expands and that causes it to turn on. The heat will cause it to retract and go off and it can go back and forth on its own. I agree that this happens. Like anything paranormal 99.9999% of the time it's bullshit. You have to make sure it's not on for longer than a few seconds before you place it. And if it starts turning on an off without you sensing something there, it's probably not paranormal. The volunteer that used this did not have it on prior to the communication. It also didn't light up immediately. There was some time before it started and some dead spots in the middle. Use your common sense, if it lights up and then off and does this consistently then it's not real. It should also never light up until instructed to.

Sarah: We've used this in every investigation since and consider it a valid tool. Many don't, and that's fine.

Joe: I firmly believe there is something to it. We've had too many experiences with it that are not random. My best example is when we lived in the house by the cemetery. The garage was haunted as fuck and I don't say that lightly. But that's a story for the next book.

The 4th floor was amazing, shadow people and communicating with spirits. And this was the first area we investigated at Waverly. We thanked the volunteer and he left to go find the other people to see if he could offer assistance to them. The four of us stood silently in the surgical room and knew that we had just experienced something together that we'd never forget. After a few moments of chit chat we knew it was time to continue to explore. Everyone else was still exploring the floors below. So we knew where to go next. We'd go up to the fifth floor.

The 5th Floor

Children's Wing

We knew from our research that the fifth floor was home to the children's wing.

Joe: I hate referring to it as a wing.

Sarah: That's what it was though.

Joe: I know, but hearing the word wing makes me hungry. I can't help it. I fucking love chicken wings. Cover them in buffalo sauce, scrumptious.

So to hear it next to the word 'children' makes me feel weird.

Sarah: You are weird.

Joe: I know. But I'm also hungry now. Shit. I'm going to have to take a break. Carry on without me.

Sarah: I'm sorry for saying this, but anything to do with the paranormal and children is just creepy. When I heard this place had a "children's wing", I knew I'd be up for it and that's why we brought a ball.

Joe: Speaking of ball, I was too lazy to get chicken wings so I just ate one of your energy balls. That sounded really dirty. I assure you it is not. Sarah makes these little balls that are good for early morning energy and also great for munching on during a ghost hunt. Fuck it, give them the recipe. I bet you don't find that in many paranormal books.

~Ghost Balls~

No bake

Ingredients:

- 1 cup rolled oats
- ½ cup chocolate chips (Dark/semi sweet is the best!)
- ½ cup crunchy peanut butter
- ½ cup ground flaxseed meal
- 1/3 cup honey or maple syrup
- 1 tsp vanilla extract
- 1 tsp ground cinnamon (optional)

Combine all the ingredients in a medium size bowl. Use a spoon to mix it together, evenly combining the ingredients together. Once that's finished, form into 1" balls using your hands (I use plastic gloves, less mess on my hands). Arrange bites on a baking sheet (you can use wax paper for an easy clean up), and freeze until they're set, which is about an hour. You're all set, go ahead and enjoy your Ghost Balls!

We get to the top of the stairs and this floor is wide open. It's covered on all sides but is different from the other floors. It's the top floor so it's much more open, lots of windows and fresh air. There were a handful of rooms, but it's more or less the roof of the building. I'm assuming they had this as the children's wing because there are parts of the wing that are wide open and at one point they had a mini playground up here.

Sarah: There used to be swing sets, slides, stuff like that for the kids to play on. Since they couldn't really leave the hospital, the roof was the next best thing for a playground. It was very roomy.

Before we do any investigating, we took a look around, surveying the area. It was crazy being there, especially so late in the evening. We step to the outside area and just look around. It is still very quiet. That's the thing about Waverly. It's so damn quiet there. The property around the facility is large so there is no exterior noise that creeps in. There were some clouds in the sky but you could see the stars really well. Looking in the distance you could see the lights from the city. But because the sanatorium is hidden by the woods, you see more trees than anything.

Sarah: It is such a surreal experience. As we're looking around we see 4 beautiful stone gargoyles that are perched up on the building. Now that's something you don't see every day. I mean, why wouldn't you have gargoyles creeping over on top of a haunted sanatorium?

As we're walking around, we couldn't help but think about all of the kids that spent time up here, knowing they can't leave and this was their home for what little time they had left. One such child seems to have never left. He is known to communicate with visitors and play with balls. His name is Timmy.

Timmy is rumored to have been a patient at Waverly and succumbed to TB around the age of six. There is a large room on the fifth floor where you will find balls lying around. They are gifts people leave for Timmy. We brought our own to leave for him in hopes that he would play with us. We set the ball down and sat around waiting to see if it would move.

We quietly discussed our experiences with each other, always keeping an eye on the ball. After a few minutes we decided to do an EVP session. We introduced ourselves to Timmy and asked if he wanted to play. We asked a few more questions and stopped the EVP session in order to continue to explore. The ball never moved while we were there. We left the room to explore a few more in the area. We still couldn't hear anyone else and assumed they were all still downstairs.

Joe: Waverly is so massive. You really have to visit to take it all in. There are rooms after rooms. Each one holds a story.

Sarah: Some of the rooms even have some history posted on the walls to read. It's on one of those that we learned about some of the doctors. Though that will come later.

After visiting a few more rooms we made our way back to where we left the ball. We were quite surprised to see that it wasn't where we left it. It was now on the other side of the room.

Sarah: I couldn't believe it. It had moved at least twenty feet.

Joe: The thing to remember with Waverly is that many of the windows are broken. We were up on the fifth floor and the higher you go the more wind there is. This makes it very possible that a gust can blow through. Plastic or rubber balls roll easily. With that being said there was no breeze coming through at that moment. I checked. We sat in the room for a short period to see if the ball would roll again. It didn't. We also didn't feel a breeze at all.

Sarah: While we didn't see or hear anyone else up there it is possible someone from another group came up and moved it. I'm pretty sure we would have heard them but that's the weird thing about Waverly. Sometimes every sound echoes. Other times it's dead silent.

Joe: What we do now when we place a ball down is to have a night vision camera placed by it in order to record any movement. We didn't do it that time because of there being other people exploring. We didn't want the camera to disappear or get stepped on.

Sarah: We decided to listen to the EVP session to see if we caught anything.

Joe: And we did.

Sarah: At the end of the EVP session we let Timmy know that we were leaving the ball for him to play with. Very quietly, in what sounds like a child's whisper, we could hear "Thank you".

Joe: The EVP mixed with the ball moving to a new place is really solid evidence. But I'm also willing to accept that someone or the wind moved the ball and possibly the "Thank you" was one of us. We always thank the spirits as we leave. None of us remember whispering "thank you", but when you are in the middle of a place like Waverly, with so much history and stimuli going around, it is possible it was said with no one remembering it. Besides, we have a much better EVP that we got later. One that caused us to all to stop dead in our tracks.

Sarah: Not exactly dead in our tracks as we were in the car driving home at the time listening to it on the stereo.

Joe: It's a figure of speech dear.

Sarah: You know I hate being called dear.

Joe: I hate being called a massive slab of manhood but you always call me that.

Sarah: I have literally never called you that.

Joe: Called me what?

Sarah: A massive slab of manhood.

Joe: Now you have and I like it. It's fitting.

502

So we left the children's wing and began to explore the rest of the 5th floor. As we walk around floor, we see a room with the numbers 502 at the top of the door.

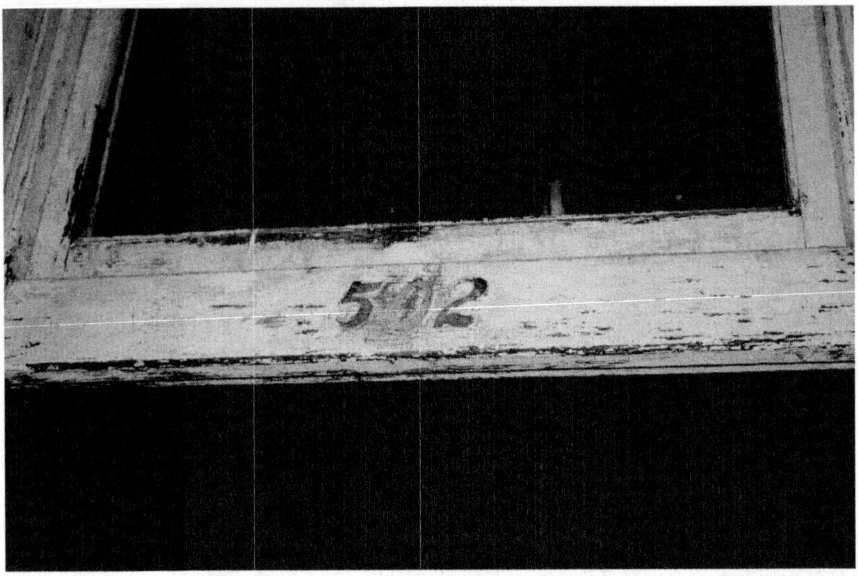

Sarah: I remember reading about this specific room. From what I understand, a nurse who worked on the 5th floor at the time, was found dead just outside room 502. She committed suicide by hanging. There is speculation but some say it was because of being unmarried and pregnant.

There are also rumors that she was murdered and hung as a cover-up. A few years later, another nurse jumped from the roof patio and fell several stories to her death. Apparently there are no records, but rumors have continued including a homeless man who was beaten to death in the room as well. Many of the rumors haven't been documented, they were just that, rumors.

Joe: There are so many urban legends regarding room 502 that it's impossible to know what's true. This is considered a hotspot in Waverly. I do know that we did an EVP session and didn't get anything.

Sarah: It felt like most of the other rooms in the sanatorium. You can't help but feel something based on the history of the place. But we didn't feel anything paranormal there.

Joe: We felt like we had to include room 502 in the book since it is one of the most known areas of the facility. I do think a nurse more than likely died there and I think she hung herself. That is the one rumor that seems to be taken as fact. All I know is we encountered nothing out of the ordinary there.

Sarah: Always remember though, spirits show themselves when they feel like it. Just because we got nothing there doesn't mean it's a hoax. It simply means we got nothing while we are there. There are tons of reports posted online of other people's experiences. I'd suggest looking them up. Many are quite fascinating.

And speaking of fascinating, we knew it was time to head to the creepiest place in the whole building, the body chute.

Body Chute aka Death Tunnel

The whole concept of the body chute is horrific. So many people died at Waverly that they created a tunnel to push the bodies down in order to not upset the patients. The tunnel is dark and long. There are steps on one side and a flat walkway on the other. It was built this way in order to push a gurney down to the bottom. At the bottom there is an exit where a transport would be to haul off the bodies.

Let it sink in. There were so many bodies that they built a tunnel to remove them from Waverly.

As we're slowly walking down flights of stairs, we take a gander down each floor as we're moving along. All the floors look very similar, long hallways with doorways and windows, with an outside balcony running the length of the building. It's interesting, each floor we visit, they all have their own feel to them. Some floors are "heavier" than others, and overall they just have a different vibe. We finally make our way down to the entrance of the body chute.

We meet up with some fellow paranormal investigators at this time and all decide to head down the chute together. Being that it was a small group of people, it helps because there's less noise and interference.

Sarah: Let me tell you, walking down this tunnel was terrifying. There were probably about 7 of us total walking down there together. Usually I feel safe with a group of people, but this night was different. Knowing what I know about this place and it being a tunnel with no windows on any sides, except a gate at the end, was very claustrophobic. It was also dusty, damp, and a bit hard to breathe.

You really have to be careful where you were walking down here. One bad step, you could go tumbling. We were walking in pitch black darkness. The only light we had was our flashlights, which came in very handy. This is a long tunnel that stretches about 425 feet, underneath the hospital.

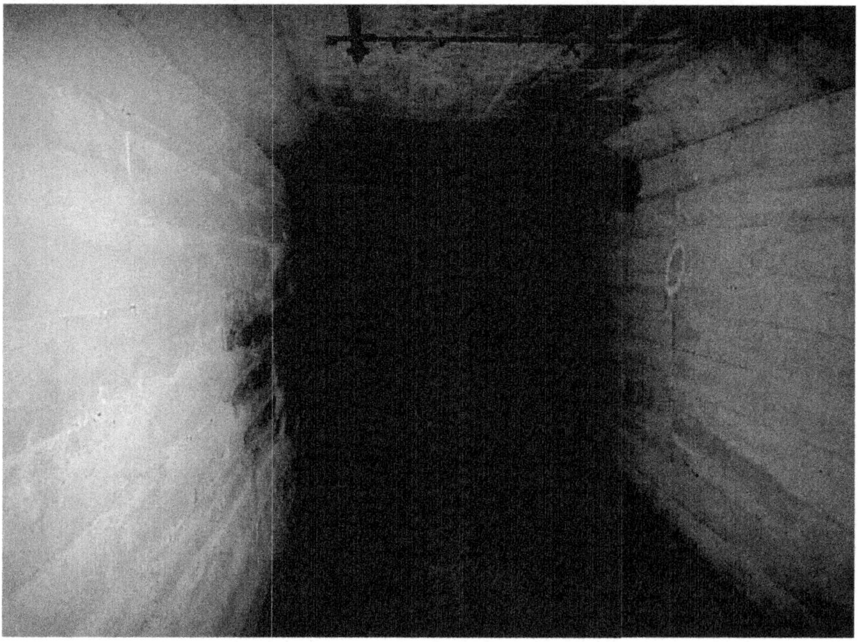

Sarah: As we're slowly walking down this "death tunnel", that's all I could think about…how many bodies were transported down here, right where I'm walking. It's very unsettling.

We all walk about half way down the tunnel and decide to try to get some EVPs.

Sarah: I thought we should be able to get some good EVPs down here considering it's so quiet.

We all sit down and just take it all in. It was about 2 or 3 am at this point, usually the prime time to catch something. A few of us start snapping some pictures while others get out their recorders and video cameras. Everyone was very respectful and quiet.

Sarah: I know I've talked about this before, but when you do investigations, sometimes you get stuff, other times you don't. There's no on and off switch when it comes to this sort of thing. You could be sitting here for hours and not get anything, you need to have patience.

Joe: That's why many people try ghost hunting and quickly give it up. There is so much down time and most of the time you'll get no paranormal experience. What you need to also focus on is the history and where you are. You are in some old buildings with so many stories. Just being there is an experience. And to get to share it with friends is amazing.

Sarah: You also have to give serious thought about the fact that you get to leave at the end of the night. Most of the people that came to Waverly never did.

Joe: That's not true. Most left right where we were, down this long, dark tunnel. I'll fully admit, it's creepy as fuck.

We start trying the flashlight out ourselves. Luckily for us our friends had brought one of the flashlights that were needed to try to communicate. It takes about 15 minutes or so, but something started to communicate with us. We went back and forth with it for a little while.

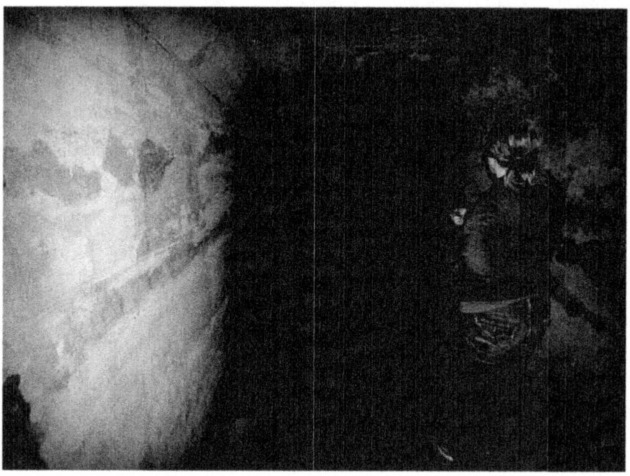

As we're doing that, others were using their voice recorders and digital cameras. A little time passes by. We decide to put the flashlight away and do some EVPS ourselves. We're all sitting there in silence.

Sarah: Out of the blue, or should I say, out of the darkness, we hear a moaning sound at the end of the tunnel. All of us hear it! It didn't last long but it sounded like a male voice moaning. We unfortunately didn't pick it up with the recorder, but we all heard it in person. We all sat there in shock. We couldn't believe what we had just heard. To make sure there was no interference, or someone wasn't playing a joke on us, someone needed to go to the end of the tunnel and investigate. There was no way in hell the 4 of us wanted to go down there. We were fine just going half ways.

Joe: I would have gone down there. I wasn't scared. I was just lazy and tired. Plus my back was hurting.

Sarah: Sure.

Joe: Actually now that I think about it, I believe I did walk 2/3's of the way down there.

Sarah: Shit, that's right.

One of the other members of the other groups decided to head down there on his own. He was fine with going by himself.

Sarah: I thought he was crazy! But without a second thought, he turned on his flashlight and slowly descended into the darkness.

We all just sat there watching him. The tunnel seems like it goes on forever. The guy gets to the end of the tunnel, looks around for a few minutes, then heads back up to us. He said the gate was locked and there was nothing down there. But while he was down there, he got goosebumps and didn't want to stay very long.

Sarah: He felt like something was watching him.

Joe: Yeah, all of us.

Sarah: I felt like that the whole time we were down there. Glad he made it back okay though, that is one brave soul!

We spend a few more minutes down there, then decide it's time to head back up and see what other trouble we can get into.

Sarah: I tell you what though, we were the first to start heading up. I didn't want to be the last one walking out of the death tunnel, nope… no way… no thank you!

Since we were on the bottom level we decided to check out that floor. We had just visited the creepiest place in the sanatorium so this floor would definitely pale in comparison. That's what we thought…but we were wrong.

The First Floor

Electroshock room

We decided to break off from the other groups and go on our own again. They had already investigated this floor so they headed up. We were very lucky to avoid the other groups for the most part. We came together a few times to share some experiences, which was very cool, but it was nice to feel like we were on our own. As we're exploring the first floor, we pass by this dark room with some old Halloween décor. Waverly has a cool Halloween haunt every year, so there's creepy décor that is kept there year round, mainly on the first floor.

Joe: When you get to Waverly you get some rules. No Ouija boards, no provoking spirits, none of that sort of thing. We were told to be respectful because you didn't want to manifest anything negative. We could leave; the volunteers and staff are there all the time so they deal with the ramifications of that stuff. You always have to remember that. You investigate, you leave. Others stay to pick up the pieces and deal with anything you happen to stir up. But here's the thing. Isn't turning a floor into a Halloween attraction with fake ghosts, monsters and people jumping out and scaring you exactly that? I certainly felt weird about that, but it's not my place to decide what is right or wrong. You'll find many dichotomies in the paranormal world and certainly this is an example of one.

Sarah: Upkeep, although minimal at Waverly is expensive. I understand that they need to make money where they can.

Joe: I'm not denying that. It just seems to be exactly the thing they warn everyone about. But it is their place so they can do what they'd like.

We walked into a decent sized room and look around. There is a large chair and a long wooden table. As we're standing there looking inside this room, the volunteer stops by to see how we're doing. We told him about the moaning in the body chute. He's heard the moaning down there too, so he was happy we got to experience that as well. He also told us about the room we were currently standing in.

Sarah: Apparently this room we stopped to look in was the electroshock therapy room.

Electroshock therapy was one of the treatments they thought would help cure TB. In the end, it killed more people then it helped. The volunteer goes on to tell us they had a group of paranormal investigators here the week before being led by a TV ghost hunting personality and in this room he decided to provoke whatever was in there.

Sarah: Which of course is a big no no. But this investigator is known for not listening.

Joe: And also for no showing at things. I won't name names here, but he was supposed to take us on a tour one time. I arranged it all as a surprise for Sarah. Of course the day before he stopped replying to messages and to this day I've never heard from him again. So it doesn't surprise me that he went in all macho and caused some issues. And no it wasn't Zak. He's a decent guy.

While provoking the spirits, the ceiling in the room started crashing down on everyone and they had to leave quickly. Whatever was residing in that room was not happy.

Sarah: The ceiling had collapsed. You could look up and see.

Joe: Whether that story was true or not, I'm not sure, but yes, the ceiling had come down. Of course parts of the building were falling apart everywhere so it is possible that it was a coincidence.

Sarah: But what about what we experienced in the room?

Joe: Well, it is possible that the negative stuff was planted in our heads simply because of the story we were told. We'll let the readers judge that.

The volunteer warned us not to stay in there too long. There is a dark entity in there, much like the Creeper on the 4th floor. Any sane person would've decided not to hang out in that room, but of course, the four of us thought we'd check it out a little longer. The volunteer wished us luck and went to check on the other groups, leaving us on our own. We decided to get the night vision camera out, along with another rubber ball we brought along. We set the camera on top of the table, turn on the night vision and point it at the ball, which we also set on the table. If the ball moves we'll be able to catch it on camera. We sat across the room on the floor to give whatever was in there space.

Joe: That's also important. I'm not sure if I mentioned it before and, well, I'm too lazy to go back to check. You should always give some space between your items and you. Give the spirits room to move and be comfortable.

We sat down and turned the flashlights off. The only thing on in the room is the camcorder.

Sarah: Let me tell you, I felt uneasy the second I walked in that room, even before the volunteer told us what happened in there the previous week. The hairs stood up on my arms. The whole time we were in there I played it as cool as possible. I didn't want to show my friends and Joe how nervous I was, so I just ran it out. I decided to get my digital voice recorder out; this was the perfect time to try to pick something up. I turned it on and we started asking questions. We usually like to try to keep the questions simple but relevant to the area we're in. We start with asking names, ages, male/female, and then we get into questions about the hospital and the electroshock therapy room. For a while we don't really get anything. It stayed pretty quiet and mellow. Joe then proceeds to ask whatever was in there to move the ball we placed on the table. Nothing happened.

We decide to try the flashlight out in the room as well. We set it up by the ball. We were getting nothing for quite some time before it finally began to interact.

Sarah: We had been in the room around thirty minutes at that point and it was silent. I had felt the heavy unease the whole time though. It finally lit up bright when we asked a certain question.

We asked if it wanted us to leave.

Joe: The flashlight lit up bright.

Sarah: Really, really bright.

We took that as a sign that it was time to move on so we stand up. We still had a lot of exploring to do around the sanitarium.

Sarah: As we're collecting ourselves, Joe decided to push it. He starts to provoke. He says stuff like I bet you can't move that ball and come out show yourself, he was getting more persuasive. I told him to stop because we don't need this kind of negative energy attaching itself to us. As he's mouthing off a bit, we all of a sudden feel a change in the room. It's hard to explain unless you've felt it before. The room becomes very heavy, breathing is a little more difficult and I knew we had to leave right away. We finish packing everything up, I turned off the recorder, and we bolt. I was not happy. Something was in there with us and we managed to piss it off.

Joe: In my defense I wasn't provoking it that much, just a little. After hearing about the ceiling crashing down I wanted to see what we could drum up.

Sarah: Yeah, not cool.

Joe: I looked at it as kind of a debunking thing.

Sarah: It worked though. You didn't debunk it of course, but you did stir something up.

Joe: Yes. The room turned quickly. It felt bad. The one thing I've learned in doing this is if it starts to feel bad, it's time to go. The heaviness is fine, you get that in many places, but there have only been a few places we've ever been that felt bad. That room was one of them. It turned quickly.

Sarah: We didn't listen to the EVP's from that room until we were driving home. We hooked the digital recorder up to the car stereo and listened to it. We wanted to mostly play the end of the recorder where Joe decided he needed to piss off the entity that was in the room with us. Right after he says, "I bet you can't move that ball", we hear a male voice say almost directly in the recorder, "Get out"! I replayed it about 3 more times and we all gasped and look up at each other without saying a word. We couldn't believe what we caught! It was amazing! To this day it's one of the best EVP's we've caught. I knew there was something in that room and knew Joe pissed it off and you can clearly hear that in the EVP!

Joe: What can I say? The room felt heavy when we first came in but we weren't getting much of a response. So when the flashlight turned on bright when we asked if it wanted us to leave I had to push it a little. It's crazy how quick the room changed though. It's still hard to believe. The EVP is creepy. The "Get Out" can be heard well.

We all heard the same thing. EVP's are tough because once you tell someone what you hear they hear it. The mind is weird that way. All four of us heard the "Get out" clearly. We almost had to pull over because of the shock.

Sarah: Something was in the room. Something that didn't want us there. Something that you pissed off.

We left that room and didn't go back. There was still many more things to explore.

The Doctor

As we're walking down the hall, we came across some old black and white hospital pictures. There were some with doctors, nurses, patients. It was really interesting to see.

Sarah: One of the pictures caught my attention. It was a tall male doctor in the typical scrubs you'd see them wearing, with a long white coat. He just stood out in my mind for some reason.

Apparently the first and second floor are known to be haunted by a spirit that resembles a doctor. People are known to see a male, full figure apparition, wearing a long white coat. Is this doctor back to perform more experiments? Has he ever left? Is this a residual haunting? We'll get back to this a little later.

Morgue

We keep heading down the hallway. We catch out of the corner of our eyes a gurney, like one from the early 40s or 50s. It was super creepy. As we turn to look at it closer, we head into this room. Low and behold it is the morgue!

Sarah: The morgue was much smaller than what I was thinking it was going to be. A single room, no bigger than a living room, with a few gurneys, sinks, and slabs you'd put bodies on. I'm not going to lie, it was creepy but awesome. I was happy to see that kind of stuff was still intact and there. If you watch some of the ghost hunting shows, people actually go inside the slabs and lie down! How nasty is that?

We heard all sorts of noises around us while in the morgue. However we were able to debunk them as people walking on the floor above. The volunteer made his way into the room with us.

Joe: We had the best of both worlds with this tour. We were on our own for the most part, but the volunteer happened to join us on a few of the key areas to fill us in with some details which were very cool.

The slabs have been shown in many paranormal shows. There are reportedly really haunted, with people being unable to lie inside for very long. They get itchy and tingly and begin to feel very uncomfortable. They hear noises coming closer and panic. This is one of the times it was great to have the volunteer there with us. We didn't have to debunk it. He did it for us as he shared the reasons why people feel what they do in there.

Waverly is an old facility. Windows are broken and there are many ways in. There is no major pest control. Small animals like to hide underneath the morgue slabs and they bring in a lot of bugs, including fleas.

Sarah: What people hear are animals. What they feel, the itchiness is generally fleas. Uh…no thank you! Plus… ewwww.

Dining hall

While on the first floor, we start meeting up with all the other groups. Together we head into this massive room with red curtains on both sides. The volunteer had us sit down for a session in this dark, red velvet curtain roped off area. Apparently this is one of the hot spots in the facility. The red curtains are part of the Halloween maze they have every year. As we sit there, people are doing EVPs, taking pictures, and doing the usual investigation type of stuff. At one point, the volunteer tells us all to be quiet and sit in the darkness. He tells us to listen. At this point all of the groups are together and no one else is walking around the facility, all the groups were in the room. Out of the blue we start hearing footsteps down the hall from us, it almost seemed like they were getting closer and closer. We hear this a couple times within a 15 minute span. Suddenly the volunteer got a worried look on his face and says we have to leave immediately that it wasn't safe.

Sarah: We of course did. I wasn't going to stay in a place that someone felt wasn't safe.

Joe: It's weird though. We heard the footsteps and saw the curtains moving a bit but the room didn't feel heavy or dark. I'm sure the curtains moved because of the wind. But he wanted us all out of the room. I trust that from his experience he knew something was going to happen. I would have loved to have stayed though.

The volunteer had a place he wanted to take all of us. It's a place we had been before, but we were fine going back again. It had been hours since we had been up to see Timmy.

The Ball

The whole group followed the volunteer up to the children's wing. This time we went into a different room. It was more open. We all sat down and the volunteer walked about thirty feet from us, set down a ball and a flashlight and came back to join us. He proceeded to begin to ask questions. The flashlight turned on almost immediately and for fifteen or so minutes came on and off. The questions were the same that we had asked and while they were interesting they aren't the reason we are talking about this area again. This time we were going to see the ball.

Sarah: Like we said before, we left a ball and though we didn't see it move, it was on the other side of the room a short time later when we came back.

Joe: We listed the reasons how it could have happened in a non-paranormal way. This time was different.

The volunteer asked Timmy to move the ball. We all sat in shocked silence as it did just that.

The ball rolled a few feet, stopped, and rolled back to the same spot.

Sarah: I couldn't believe it.

Joe: Me neither. I had to debunk it.

When the group all dispersed we stayed. The room is surrounded by broken windows so wind blows in. We didn't feel any breeze while we were up there, but that doesn't mean there wasn't one. We walked to where he set the ball. There were no grooves there. Nothing that the ball was in that could facilitate movement. We checked the windows and felt no air.

Joe: It's bizarre. Even if wind caused it to move it wouldn't have rolled back to the same spot. I couldn't figure it out.

Sarah: It was Timmy.

Joe: It was something. I fully believe something up there moved the ball. Whether it was Timmy I don't know.

Sarah: We should add that we couldn't get this on video. Our camera suddenly stopped working on that floor. There should have been plenty of juice left in it. It has a ten hour charge and we had only had it on for an hour or so.

Joe: As you read in the last book, you did read the last one right? If not, you should, it's a fun read. Unless you don't like this one. If this style of conversation writing doesn't appeal to you the other book won't be something you'll like. You should still buy it to support us of course…just don't read it. As I was saying, we talked in the last book about our camera dying in the Salem cemetery and then coming back on when we left. This was similar, though the camera never came back on until we plugged it back in.

Sarah: I wish we could have captured this. It was amazing and while some of the other rooms felt dark, this one didn't. It felt playful which is why I'm convinced it was a child we were communicating with.

We left that area and found ourselves walking along a hallway with large windows that looked outside. These large hallways were built in order to wheel the beds out so the patients could get sun. Most the windows are broken but looking out in the early morning was quite striking.

Sarah: It's amazing how calm you end up feeling in Waverly.

Joe: It's also amazing how quick you get the layout down. By the end of the night we could navigate that place like we'd been there for years.

Good Mourning

The sun was starting to come up. It was really pretty seeing the sunrise while in Waverly Hills. It's a beautiful view being surrounded with trees and the peacefulness of it all. We can see why they chose the spot they did to build this hospital. It's quiet and hidden from the world.

Sarah: I really hope this view provided some comfort for those that spent the last of their days at Waverly. I can't imagine what it was like for them.

Joe: Standing there, with Sarah, and with our friends we were thankful for the experiences we've had, and those we would continue to have. We are lucky. Many were not.

At this point it was getting close to the end of the 8 hour investigation. We decide to take a walk outside the building to snap some pictures.

What a majestic place. You really don't realize how big it is until you see it in person. It looms over the whole valley. We get back to the gift shop to buy a few things and say our goodbyes. As we're walking out back to the car Veronica snaps a few more pictures of the outside. The place feels much different during the day than it does at night, naturally I guess. It was great seeing the sanitarium in the morning light. You can really get some good shots of the building from the outside. Plus it doesn't feel as ominous. It's not scary during the day, it's more sad.

We get in the car and do a once over. We say our goodbyes and do a quick little ritual which includes:

"Thank you for having us here. We had a great time. This was a lovely place to visit. Please do not follow us home. You have to stay here."

We try to be respectful but at the same time stern. We've heard horror stories of entities following people home and not leaving. We didn't want that to happen, especially from here. As we're driving back to the hotel to get some shut eye before our long journey home, we look over the last few pictures we took. Veronica yelled out to us. She couldn't believe what she was seeing.

Sarah: She handed the camera to me to show me what she caught. I look at the camera and couldn't believe what I was seeing. On the second floor we see a tall man dressed in a white jacket. I couldn't believe it! That had to be the doctor we seen in the pictures! It looked just like him. What a catch on her part!

First is the full size image. Look all the way to the right, third window down.

Now we'll zoom in on the window. The quality isn't very good and I have no idea what it will look like printed but we see what appears to be a man in white.

We know that there was no one on the tour dressed like that. All four of us immediately thought of the Doctor from the picture. We have been unable to debunk it.

Final Thoughts

Sarah

This trip was amazing and I can't wait to get back to Waverly to experience this all over again. The things we experienced here will stay with me forever. Since then, Joe and I have done many more investigations over the years and have really learned a lot. We want to come back here to put some of our skills to the test and hopefully catch more stuff. Let me tell you, if you're into the paranormal, Waverly is one place you have to visit! They call Waverly Hills Sanatorium the most haunted place on earth… for a reason.

Joe

If you're into the paranormal then Waverly Hills sanatorium should be number one on your list of places to see. I have zero doubt in my mind that it is haunted. We had far too many experiences there for it to be anything else. While Salem is the place that I began to believe in the paranormal, Waverly is the place where it truly came alive for me. It's a massive structure full of so many horrible and sad moments for people. It can't help but retain some of that. I've also retained something from Waverly, the shadow people. This was my first experience seeing the shadow people. Since then I have seen them many other times. I'm not sure whether that is because of seeing spirits at Waverly, or whether it's because the spirits seen me. I do know that once we got back home to Rochester, I began to experience things in our house. I don't know if something followed me back, but something took notice of me and it wasn't always nice. You'll be able to read all about it in our next book coming out in October 2018.

Haunted Journeys: The House on 6th Street

Joe Knetter is a horror writer from Minnesota now living in Los Angeles, California.

Sarah French is an actress from Minnesota now living in Los Angeles, California.

Brainwaves horror and paranormal talk radio

Spooky, funny, touching, honest, offensive, and at times completely random, *Brainwaves* airs live every Wednesday evening beginning at 8:00 PM Pacific Time (11:00 midnight Eastern Time)

Knetter and Creepy will be taking your calls LIVE and unscreened via Skype, so let your freak flags fly! Feel free to add **BrainWavesTalk** to your Skype account so you can reach us, or call in from a landline or cellphone – **858 480 7789**. The duo also take questions via Twitter; you can reach us at **@BrainwavesRadio** or **@UncleCreepy**, **@JoeKnetter**. Have news you think we should be talking about? Then hit up the Dark and Bark News Team **@MrDarkDC** and **@JonathanBarkan** using **#BrainWaves**.

Have a ghost story or a paranormal story but can't call in? Feel free to email it to me directly at **UncleCreepy@dreadcentral.com** with "*Brainwaves Story*" in your subject line. You can now become a fan of the show via the official... **BRAINWAVES FACEBOOK PAGE**!

Brainwaves: Horror and Paranormal Talk Radio is hosted live (with shows to be archived as they progress) right here on Dread Central. You can tune in and listen via the FREE TuneIn Radio app or listen to **TuneIn right through the website**!

For more information and to listen live independent of TuneIn, visit the **Deep Talk Radio Network website**, "like" **Deep Talk Radio on Facebook**, and follow **Deep Talk Radio on Twitter**. And don't forget to subscribe to *Brainwaves* on iTunes.

Printed in Dunstable, United Kingdom

73435872R00077